THE ADVENTURES OF
STELLA & WALTER

DEDICATION

To all of my students -- if it weren't for
each and every one of you, I would never
have followed my dream of writing a
children's book. Thank you for inspiring
me every single day.

TABLE OF CONTENTS

WALTER

Walter was a good dog. He loved his family. He loved his home. He loved his bed. He loved his yard.

Everyday he woke up, stretched, and greeted his humans.

He went outside to make sure the yard was squirrel-free and to leave his humans presents.

Then he would eat, sleep, and play the rest of the day! He loved playing frisbee with his humans and cuddling on his favorite green chair most of all!

Life was PAWS-ATIVELY awesome!

UNTIL...

His humans got a new dog.

"Walter, meet your new friend Stella!"
they said. *Bleh!* thought Walter.

"You're going to love her!" they said.
Bleh, bleh! thought Walter.

"It will be fun to have a new friend to
play with!" they said.
Bleh, Bleh, Bleh! thought Walter.

Stella was big, fluffy, and looked way
too happy in Walter's opinion.

STELLA

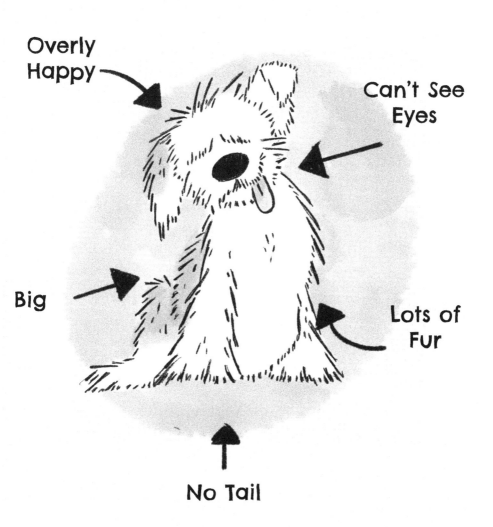

Overly Happy

Can't See Eyes

Big

Lots of Fur

No Tail

MEETING STELLA

"Hi there!" barked Stella.

Walter just looked at her.

Stella came up and sniffed him.

Walter just looked at her.

"Wanna play?" asked Stella.

Walter just looked at her.

"We can play chase, tag, hide and seek..." said Stella. "I don't want to play!" huffed Walter. He started to walk away.

pant pant pant...

"STOP FOLLOWING ME!" barked Walter.

"STOP FOLLOWING ME!" barked Stella.

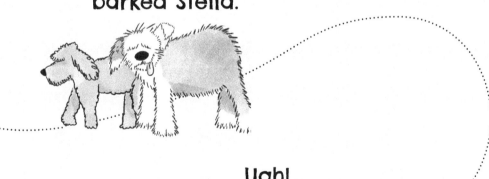

Ugh!

"STOP COPYING ME!"
howled Walter.

"STOP COPYING ME!"
howled Stella.

"PINEAPPLE GHOST
BANANAS!"
yipped Walter.

"PINEAPPLE GHOST
BANANAS!"
yipped Stella.

"Ugh," face-pawed Walter. It's going to

be a long day.

WALTER

Perfect hair

Thin

Prances

Athletic

D(

Fast

Loud

9

STELLA

Giant Fluff

Slow

Thick

Clumsy

GS

Quiet

Hops

THE BACKYARD

"Why don't you two go outside and play?" the humans asked.

"I don't want her in MY backyard!" Walter whined. But the humans let them both out anyway.

"WOW!" barked Stella. "This backyard is...

PAW FECT!

It is pretty paw-fect, thought Walter. He decided he was going to do his normal Walter routine. Maybe she would leave him alone!

Walter walked the perimeter.

Walter barked at the squirrels.

BORKETY BORK!

BARK! BARK!

Walter rolled on his back to sunbathe.

"Don't you have something better to do than follow me?" asked Walter.

"NOPE!" barked Stella.

"Fine," said Walter. "Let me at least show you the RIGHT way."

RULES
OF THE YARD

1. PATROL THE PERIMETER

2. BARK AT SQUIRRELS

3. ROLL IN A GOOD PATCH OF GRASS

4. SUNBATHE

5. REPEAT

"We're going to practice the rules now, Stella," said Walter. "Kapeesh?"

"Kaposh!" said Stella.

"First you must patrol the perimeter of the yard," he said.

"Perimeter?" asked Stella.

"The edges, along the fence," said Walter.

"Now, bark at all squirrels," said Walter.

BARK!
BARK!

"And roll properly, side to side," said Walter.

"So, how did I do?" asked Stella.

"Not bad for a fluff ball," said Walter.

"Woof-hoo!! Can we play a game now?" pleaded Stella.

"I guess," said Walter, tail wagging.

"Let's play tag," said Stella.

"Okay," said Walter. "You're it!" he said, pawing Stella on the nose. "Catch me if you can!"

Stella and Walter played for a long time until they were both too tired to keep running!

"Now what?" panted Stella.

"Nap time," panted Walter.

"Alright," panted Stella. They both yawned.

Just as Walter was about to fall asleep he heard Stella say, "Sweet dreams, best friend."

"You too, Stella," yawned Walter. *Maybe she isn't so bad*, thought Walter as he fell asleep.

NAP TIME

ZZZZZ...

THE PARK

Walter jumped up and wagged his tail. He LOVED going to the park. There was so much to do there!

Jungle Gym!

Splash Pad!

Slides!

Basketball court!

Stella and Walter got their leashes and walked with their humans to the park.

As they walked, Stella kept running into Walter and pushing him off the sidewalk.

"Hey!" snapped Walter. "Could you stop pushing me off the sidewalk?!"

"Oops! Sorry!" cried Stella. "I don't mean to push you off, but I am a herding dog! I naturally push animals in certain directions!"

"Well knock it off!" said Walter.

"I'll try," said Stella.

When they finally got to the park, Walter didn't know what to do first!

"Race you to the top!" howled Stella as she hopped past him toward the jungle gym.

As if she could beat me, thought Walter, as he raced after her. He gracefully ran past her, jumped up the stairs, and was about to yell down to Stella when he heard a voice.

"Hey, you! No hybrids allowed!"

Walter turned around and saw a perfectly groomed Poodle looking at him.

"Oh! Hi!" started Walter, tail wagging, but the Poodle cut him off and rolled her eyes.

"I said, NO hybrids allowed."

"What's a hybrid?" panted Stella who had just caught up. She noticed that Walter's ears drooped and his tail stopped wagging.

"A hybrid is someone like HIM," sneered the Poodle. "He's half Golden Retriever and half Poodle."

"What's wrong with that?" demanded
Stella, confused.

"Look at him! He's not like you and me.
We are purebred dogs. We are perfect. He
is not," said the Poodle. "You better get off
this jungle gym or..."

"Or what?" said Stella, standing up taller.
"The park is here for everybody, no matter
what they look like."

"Walter is funny, fast, nice, and a good protector! Who cares if he is a hybrid," said Stella.

"Hmph!" snorted the Poodle, not looking at them.

"C'mon Walter," said Stella. "We can go play basketball instead."

Walter wagged his tail again and smiled at Stella. "Okay," he said, "but only if we race there!"

Stella started to hop away, but Walter turned
to the Poodle.

"You can come too, if you want," said Walter.
"We can always use more players."

Then Walter raced after Stella toward the
basketball court.

"Time to go home!" cried the humans.

Stella and Walter were tired and ready to go. As they walked home, Stella pushed into Walter.

"Oops!" said Stella. "I'm sorry for herding you again."

"It's okay," said Walter. "I don't mind so much."

Stella smiled. "I hope we can have another adventure together soon!" she said.

Walter wagged his tail. "Me too."

THE END

Paw-some Facts

GOLDENDOODLES

Mix of Golden Retrievers and Poodles (hybrid).

Good family dogs.

Agile

Intelligent

Social

Friendly

Loyal

Energetic

Paw-some Facts

OLD ENGLISH SHEEPDOGS

Herding dogs - work to herd sheep and cattle.

Nicknamed "Bob-tail" since their tails are often

short and stubby.

Bubbly

Even-tempered

Playful

Social

Loving

ABOUT STELLA AND WALTER

Stella and Walter are actually best friends in real life! They love spending time together and getting into all kinds of trouble! The both live in Ohio with their humans and spend as much time together as possible.

Stella is extremely lovable and funny. She likes rolling in the grass, and she LOVES Walter.

Walter is very smart and energetic. He loves to run around outside and hang out with his mom.

Stella and Walter's relationship inspired their human to write a story about all the adventures they might go on together if they had the chance!

CPSIA information can be obtained
at www.ICGtesting.com
Printed in the USA
LVHW070909041119
636223LV00030B/428/P